the
Perfect
Journey

The second *The Guardian*/Piccadilly
Writing Competition for Teenagers,
The Perfect Journey?, received a tremendous
response. The entries were imaginative,
clever and varied, and the panel of judges
– Michael Palin (author, film and TV star),
Rosie Rushton (author and journalist) and
Joanna Carey (author, reviewer and
feature writer for *The Guardian*) – faced a
difficult task. The winning stories,
by Laura Barnett, Fatema Begum,
Dominic Burgess, Leigh Debbage,
Nikki Dudley, Laura Gordon,
Jennifer Haddon, Michael Hallsworth,
Edmund Hunt and Joanna Morris, display
great talent, insight and maturity, and the
different struggles and challenges they
explore make this a memorable
collection of journeys.

the Perfect journey

Winners of The Guardian/Piccadilly teenage writing competition

Piccadilly Press • London

First published in Great Britain in 2000
by Piccadilly Press Ltd,
5 Castle Road, London NW1 8PR

A catalogue record for this book is available
from the British Library

ISBNs: 1 85340 691 0 (hardback)
1 85340 696 1 (trade paperback)

1 3 5 7 9 10 8 6 4 2

Printed and bound by Bookmarque Ltd

Set in 11.5pt Meridien

Cover design by Judith Robertson

Contents

Foreword	7
Sticks and Stones LAURA BARNETT	9
The Mehndi of My Love FATEMA BEGUM	19
It's a Compromise Anyway DOMINIC BURGESS	33
Smorgasbord LEIGH DEBBAGE	47
Playing With Fate NIKKI DUDLEY	61
Tam LAURA GORDON	69
Departures JENNIFER HADDON	83
Relativity MICHAEL HALLSWORTH	89
Out of Darkness EDMUND HUNT	105
Your Last Cigarette JOANNA MORRIS	117

Foreword

Michael Palin

I had a great deal of fun reading and assessing the stories for this competition. It was not only exciting to read such rich variety in the stories, but it was also highly encouraging to see so much teenage talent! I felt, however, that although I was on the panel with Joanna Carey of *The Guardian* and author Rosie Rushton, as a travel writer, I should have been a psychologist! So many of the entries dealt with journeys of the mind rather than the sort of travelling I indulge in. This made the judging even more rewarding.

Congratulations to all the winners! Having your story published at such a young age is a wonderful achievement, and I think the reader will find that all ten authors have been true to themselves, and written with flair and individuality. The book, as a whole, is a wonderful read.

Michael Palin

Sticks and Stones

Laura Barnett

Sticks and Stones

I lie motionless in my cocoon, suspended in time. All normal milestones of the day have gone, replaced by others alien to my own, imposed upon me by impersonal hands in surgical gloves. Everything is pale; the bed, the walls, the light. My skin is so thin and tight that it is almost translucent. I feel it is holding my bones together, like those babies born unformed. I feel pure, purged, empty, as if I am hollow.

But what worries me most is how empty my mind is. Words and images flutter past like litter cast by the breeze, dissolving as soon as they appear. I cannot pin them down. I wonder if perhaps my soul has left me and my body, a dry husk, is functioning on auto-pilot.

I wasn't always obsessive, of course. I can remember when it started, can trace the process. It seems there was a process. How else does one change from a perfectly normal human being to one caged, trapped by her own perceptions? If I focus, a little at a time, on how I came to be here, perhaps I will be able to answer their questions with sincerity, not only telling them what they want to hear, repeating textbook answers. So that's why I'm talking to you now, machine. To try to get my mind back. To take a step back along this journey to 'perfection'. This perfect journey.

Nine years old. Body changing. Suddenly it is no longer subject to one's requirements. It seems to develop a mind of its own. I mark this as the beginning. I do not recollect being aware of my body before then.

Changing in the girls' toilets after Games.

'How much do you weigh?' Natasha asks Sabrina.

Sabrina smiles. 'Six and a half stone. Mummy wonders how I don't blow away in the breeze.'

'How about you, Georgina?' Natasha turns to me.

'Nine.'

'Nine stone?' Everyone seems to be listening, all faces are intent upon me. I feel my cheeks glow red.

'You must be very fat,' says Sabrina. All eyes appraise me critically. For the first time I am ashamed of my body, and I fear the scales.

Ten years old. The word 'male' suddenly develops connotations. They are different beings, a fact emphasised when they are sent out of the classroom while the teacher shows us the sanitary towels that she keeps in the cupboard for our use. When the boys are allowed back in they cower sheepishly in the corner, smothering their embarrassment with sniggers. We feel aloof, superior, united in our femininity.

'Oh yes, madly.'

'I wouldn't touch her if you paid me.'

'That's what I thought.' She laughs.

Tears, humiliation. He does not need to voice the reason why. My size is a barrier. I can only conclude that I am a 'fat person', pigeonholed forever, regardless of brainpower or the contents of my imagination. Image is everything. I desire desperately to fit in, to achieve 'perfection', a notion which I carry in my mind like a yardstick to which I cannot measure up. How can I? Never until I shed these pounds.

Fifteen and desperate. The food which I have always loved becomes odious; I see it only in terms of fat and calories, calories which I may never burn off. I loathe exercise; my cheeks flush red as beetroots and I am continuously aware of how I must look. A whale in a tracksuit: ridiculous. So if I cannot burn the calories, I must stop them entering my body.

I begin to connect the food on my plate with my weight, and it obsesses me. Everywhere models promote the size that I should be, that everyone else seems to have attained. Food becomes a symbol of the burden which I carry. So I stop eating.

It's hard at first. I watch the others scoffing plates of chips with envy, but secretly I am smug. For now I know that I can become like them, that soon I will have the figure I crave. And avoiding meals is not difficult; my mother gets home too late from work to cook me dinner, so I just tell her I made myself something. To stop the pangs occasionally I have a water biscuit, and I drink a lot of mineral water. I feel pure, powerful.

The weight comes off easily. After a few weeks I have lost a stone. I weigh myself at least twice a day and check my shoulders in the mirror to see if the bones are protruding. At school somebody comments, 'Georgina, you've lost so much weight.' It is Frances, the slimmest and most beautiful girl in the class.

'Yeah, you look great,' her equally stick-like friend Kate adds.

I am determined to continue. And when Tom sees the new, thinner me, and asks me out, I know that I will not stop.

However, soon it is not a matter of not wanting to stop. I cannot stop. Two stone, three stone, dropping like dead birds from the sky. I feel like I'm on a roller-coaster, a runaway train with no brakes. I try to eat something and throw up. This is controlled by my brain no longer. My body has taken over.

Of course Mum soon notices, and the girls at school. They tell me I look like a skeleton, but I look in the mirror and see only the rolls of fat, the critical, disapproving looks of the girls in the changing-room and the mocking faces of Sam and Richard, feel the isolation of the fat girl nobody wanted to partner in the dance lesson. They all tell me I have to eat, but they don't realise that I can't. There is no escape. To be thin and perfect is my goal; until I reach it, I will not stop, and I do not yet feel that I have neared it.

And then one day my body gives up. I am sitting in a Maths lesson at school when black spots begin to dance before my eyes. The spots become larger, whirling and twisting like images in a kaleidoscope, finally focusing into one mass of colourless matter. Everything goes black.

So that's how I got here. They brought me in while I was unconscious, so I couldn't fight. And now I feel so numb that there is no fight left in me.

Still my body refuses food. Vomit has become a part of everyday existence. My white cocoon encircles me, protecting me. They will not let me have a mirror, but I know that I'm still fat, that even if my ribs are showing, the fatness lurks inside, waiting to seize the moment to return.

But maybe things will get better now. The butterflies in my mind are beginning to settle. Memory is flooding back. I am retracing the steps of my journey from this place of respite. I only wish I knew where I was going now.

The Mehndi of My Love

Fatema Begum

The Mehndi of My Love

A wind rustled the tree branches. The window creaked and the curtain flapped restlessly. I sat silently on top of the bed, my arms wrapped round my legs. I could hear the wind rippling the waters of the pond, just outside my room. A slow breeze brushed past me, taking with it the scarf from my head. I got off the bed and stood in front of the mirror. My face looked pale and tired. I sat down and did a long plait at the back of my hair. The noise in the house was dying down a bit. Guests were leaving and only the closest ones were staying back, to make more preparations for tomorrow. I looked at my hands. The colour of the *mehndi* was a deep brown and it was designed like a flower, a very delicate thing. I've heard that on those who love their partner very much, the colour sticks. That is only a superstition but I know in reality who I love very much. I promised my one love, Maroof, that on these nights I wouldn't punish or torture myself. Living a life without you is more than a torture. Why did we get separated? Isn't our love strong enough to keep us together? There was a knock on my door.

'Rani? Rani, let me in, *beta*. I want to talk to you for some time. Rani?'

It was my grandma. I went to open the door.

'My child, look at you. I've noticed you haven't been eating your food properly these days. Have you read the *Maghrib namaz* yet?'

I nodded my head as a yes.

'Go and sit down while I bring some food for you.'

The decorating was still going on. The ladies started to sing wedding songs and the girls were deciding how to dress up for tomorrow. I went over to the window to look at the view from my room. A damp wind blew from the east as I looked up to the billions of stars looking down on me. What are you doing now? Are you thinking about me? Tomorrow, I shall belong to someone else. A drop of rain fell on my cheek. I brushed it away. Your touch is gone, but what a touchstone you have left within my heart. Your touch is so slender, your voice so gentle . . .

'Rani, here is your food. *Beta*, let me feed you one last time tonight. You will leave us all tomorrow and I'll have no one to feed then, nor someone to tell me off whenever I . . .'

'Grandma, please don't cry.'

I gave her a big hug. I removed her tears and kissed her forehead, like she had always done to me. She started to feed me and I then drank some water and lay down with my head on her lap. She started to stroke my hair.

'Rani, listen to what I am saying very carefully.

After tomorrow, you will belong to someone else. You will go to your proper house now and you will be put in charge of many responsibilities. Don't ever let your in-laws down and always listen to your husband. Love them all dearly like you always did here, *beta*, and don't forget us. Do write letters or phone whenever you can.'

'Is he coming tomorrow?'

'Who?'

'Maroof.'

'*Astaghfirullah*! What are you saying? You shouldn't be even thinking about any other man in that manner right now apart from your husband. Rani, my dear, don't try to remember the past and bring it to the future. What's gone is gone. Think about what's going to happen and how you should keep your husband happy.'

'How can you tell me to forget him? I can't. I can't forget him. He was my first love and the last.'

'You will have to learn to love your husband. All partners learn to love each other and build up the trust between them so that their relationship can stay strong.'

'We only fell in love. We didn't do a sin. We said we'd walk this path together, hand in hand, and support each other when in need. How am I going to walk the right path of this journey without him? A stranger . . . how can I trust a stranger to show me

23

the right path? He doesn't even know how my journey began!'

'Stop it, Rani. Finish this argument now and listen to me. Being born is like a gift from *Allah*, and we have to start from the beginning of this journey right to the end when we die. Everyone in their lives walks this journey of life. And after you get married, your support comes along, and you have to learn to trust and love each other, no matter what. Look at all the generations behind you in your family. Has anyone ever got stuck anywhere or complained about anything they were not happy about? No, *na*? Your parents have done their best for you and I've seen the boy. He makes an excellent match and is very well-mannered. Now go to sleep as you have to wake up early tomorrow.'

I began to sob and lay down on her lap again, as she stroked my hair. Tears were running down my hot cheeks. I could hear the tinkling of the raindrops outside and the wind had faded away, just like it had two years ago . . .

I still remember that afternoon. From time to time the rain would slacken, then a gust of wind would madden it again. I had to return a book to the library and by the time I got there my white laced *shalwar kameez* was soaked with rain. Not even my scarf could hide the skin showing through. I handed the book in and as I turned around, I saw one of my aunties.

The Mehndi of My Love

'*Assalamu-alaikum, auntiji.*'

'*Walaikum assalam.* How are you, *beta*? Come to return books? How is Rahul your brother these days? Heard he's gone to university to study law?'

'Yes, he's fine and he is studying law. Hopefully to become a lawyer.'

'A successful lawyer. You know your father doesn't settle for second best where his reputation is concerned. Well, I'll be going now. Give my *Salam* to everyone at home.'

I turned around and started to walk. What right did she have to interfere in my family business? Some people . . . Ouch! In rage I bumped into someone and all I could see were papers all over the floor. That was the first step in the path to happiness. It began with him. As we both picked up all the papers scattered on the floor, we ended up holding the last paper together, and that's when I first met his gaze. His eyes were hazel with a twinkle in them.

'Hi, I'm Maroof. What's your name?'

'I'm . . . I'm . . . My name is Rani. Here's your p-paper and I'm really sorry about this.'

'Oh, it's OK. It's not really your fault. I should've been careful where I was walking. I'm just new in this area and you are the first person I've made friends with so far. Well, I've got an admission to the city college and . . .'

'Oh, have you? I mean, that's good. It is a good college and I'm also attending it.'

'Excellent! So, er, we can talk to each other now. Friends?'

He offered to shake my hand. I accepted it.

'Friends.'

'By the way, if you're not doing anything would you . . . erm . . . like to have a cup of coffee with me? I know it's raining but at least the wind's faded away . . .'

My eyes fill with sleep and from time to time I wake up thinking of what fate has in store for me tomorrow and also about you. I look at you in my mind now. I can still see that sweet smile of yours and the twinkle in your eyes. When I think about that moment when we first met, I think that my life's flow never stopped at any one spot until I met you, and now I think, can this journey of life and love ever continue without you? Our hopes, our aims, what will become of them? Hopes are only there to give you a feeling that there is a chance, something can happen. Right now what do I want? Should I marry the person whom my parents have chosen for me or the person I dream of being with for the rest of my life? Dreams, they only come true when you are dreaming and not in reality. In reality what should I do? My parents have done so many good things for me and this thing that they are doing is also for my happiness, so why can't I sacrifice a small thing for them? But . . . but how can I learn to forget Maroof? He is my love. Oh, I can't bear it. It hurts my soul. I think I will go ahead with the wedding and see what happens. I lay beside my grandma and fell asleep gradually into the dawn of the next morning.

At the first rays of the sun the very next morning, everyone woke up and got busy straight away. All the decorations in the house were hung up, all the cooking was being done now and you could smell the sweet aroma of the spices in the air. I wore a very heavily embroidered sari. The wide gold border of my dark red sari fell circling my feet. The end of my sari was wound tightly across my chest and draped over my shoulders, leaving the *pallu* to hang. The gold jewellery I wore was ancient in design and the pieces were beautifully crafted. Finally, a big *dupatta* was put on top of my head, slightly covering my face and helping me to hide my embarrassment and tears in front of everyone.

I sat on top of the bed in my room, my head facing downwards, and everyone was gathered round me, all glimmering in wedding colours. My mum came into the room with a tray full of *lodhra* and jasmine flowers. The fragrance of these flowers hugged the air in the room and it smelled beautiful. She put the flowers down and asked everyone to leave the room. A mother-to-daughter talk was coming up.

'*Mashallah*! My daughter looks very beautiful today. It is as if the moon has been captured and dressed up, waiting to shine against the dark night.'

She sat next to me and kissed my forehead. I could hear the faint crying in her voice.

'I just want you to know that you have been a very good daughter to us. You have made us proud parents and we love you very much . . .'

'Oh, Ma!'

I hugged her tightly and we were both crying, letting our sorrows flow out, never to return again. At that moment my brother came into the room.

'Ma, Salma aunty wants the flowers so she . . . Wow! You look pretty today. What's this? I can see tears in your eyes? I think you should save them for when you see your husband later on! Ha!'

'Ma, tell him . . .'

'Rahul, don't upset your sister now. She is going to leave us very soon.'

'OK, OK. I'm sorry, Sis.'

He came over and gave me a kiss on the cheek. After that they left the room and closed the door behind them.

The window was wide open and a gush of breeze brushed past me, tinkling the silver bangles on my hand. There was rustling in the tree. I could hear whispers. Who or what is it? I went over to the window and just at that moment I saw Maroof walking past the house. He stopped outside. My heart was beating fast and I was in shock at seeing him. It was as if the wind had carried my message to my beloved and brought him here.

Oh Maroof, I thought, I still love you and I miss you so much!

I remembered how it had felt to be held tightly in his arms that last time we were together. If I climbed out of the window to join him, we could run away right now and live happily ever after. But then I realised that this was only a dream built up by my hopes. I can't let my parents down now. They've been there my whole life, only wanting my happiness, and supporting me no matter what.

Why, why would I want to do something now that is out of our tradition and would ruin my parents' lives? They have sacrificed so much for me, why can't I just do this for them? You need courage to be able to follow your true found path. And I don't have the courage to leave behind my whole family.

'I'll always remember you, Maroof. Farewell, my love!' I whispered to myself.

'Rani! Open the door quickly. The groom is here and everyone's going to greet him . . . Rani?'

'Yeah . . . erm . . . I'll be down in ten minutes.'

I couldn't help it but I started to cry again. I could

hardly say anything. I just stood there, looking at him, my eyes dim.

'Rani, are you coming out?'

I quickly removed my tears and went out of the room, accompanied by my friends. The house was full with people, and everywhere you looked they were glimmering in evening colours. I was standing in front of the groom by now, my gaze kept down, and I had to put a garland round his neck. It was his turn now. I lifted my head a little and as he was putting the garland round my neck, he smiled a little. I couldn't help it but the corners of my lips lifted a bit as well.

Everyone seemed very happy and they were cheering.

There was a red carpet set out in front of us and we had to walk this path together, up to the two big chairs at the top. We were walking together and flowers were being sprinkled on us. How happy everyone seemed to be! Even I haven't been so sad since I have met the new love of my life, my husband. I thought my journey was going to be incomplete, until I met you and now I think, maybe, just maybe, we could find a path that could lead us both through our perfect journey in life. Maybe, just maybe, love's journey has begun now . . .

Glossary

Allah: The name for God in the Islamic religion

Assalamu alaikum: Greetings and salutation of Muslims, meaning peace be upon you

Astaghfirullah: Meaning have shame, or a sign of exclamation

Bangle: A large ring worn on arms/legs

Beta/Beti: Son/Daughter. Also means dear, e.g. 'come here, dear'

Dupatta: A length of cloth covering the head (like a scarf)

Jasmine: A shrub with white or yellow, sweet-smelling flowers

Lodhra flowers: Flowers in the winter

Maghrib: Evening prayer offered just after sunset

Mashallah: Say this on something good done or seen

Mehndi/henna: A reddish dye taken from a plant for colouring hands, feet, hair etc.

Namaz: Prayer

Pallu/pallav: Open end of the sari which hangs on left shoulder

Salam: Greeting

Sari/saree: Length of cotton or silk worn as main garment by women

Shalwar Kameez: *Shalwar* are loose trousers and a

kameez is an overdress, both worn together
Walaikum-assalam: Response to a greeting, meaning
peace be upon you too

It's a Compromise Anyway

Dominic Burgess

It's a Compromise Anyway

Deep inside the throbbing heart of the warm, gentle building lies an old man. He rests upon his bed, snug between the fresh, comforting quilts, clinging to them as if to save himself from descending into an abyss. He looks for all the world like a foetus, safe inside his mother's womb, free from the failures of his life.

The old man has spent what seems like an eternity lying in the bed, as silent as a ghost and as still as a forgotten lake. He turns occasionally, though only to relieve the monotony, not to escape from his pain – he learned long ago that nothing could free him from that.

Sometimes he remembers being outside, though only vaguely. Reaching down to smell a rose, its sweet perfume filling his heart with joy, then rolling on the grass, feeling its hands softly tickling his face. Sometimes he can still feel the sun warming his skin, watching him, illuminating his life; can feel the wind stroking his face compassionately, as a mother might do. Other times he convinces himself that he has never left the comforting grasp of this bed.

Today the weather outside is bitter and harsh. Angry hailstones ram into the windows and create a nasty chill, spreading discomfort as far as is possible. And the wind forces itself between the gaps in the frail old structure, whispering obscenities into the old man's ears and rattling the windows, a mother who doesn't love her child.

People come and go in the home, nurses mostly. They soothe him, encourage him, though it is only reluctantly that he'll leave his fortress. The nurses are blonde and beautiful; life glows in their bright blue eyes. Life that is so obviously absent in the mirror.

'Come on, David,' they say to him.

'Yeah, come on, Davey. It's your go.'

Davey, hands trembling violently, blood pumped by fear flowing through him, grabbed hold of the rope. The wind billowed through his baggy clothes, blowing his long hair in a hundred different directions all at once.

If I close my eyes, this will all go away, thought Davey. But it didn't. Like a stubborn mule, set in its ways, the situation refused to fade out. He was still clinging on to the makeshift rope slide, the wind still pushing against him, the ravine still raging miles below at the foot of the mountain.

The other boys, still glaring at him from across the river, their eyes like jagged metal, enjoyed the perverse delight of seeing someone suffer.

'Hurry up, Davey. Or are you too wet?'

Whoosh!

With a thump Davey landed on the ground, his young, fragile body rolling across the clinging mud. Still not daring to open his eyes.

'Nice one, Davey!'

Gingerly, he opened his eyes, seeing first his tiny trainers, laces still dancing with the wind. Then, with a swift movement, he leaped to his feet. He felt twice his usual height, felt like an action hero, like somebody important.

Head held high, he glanced around the small crowd of boys, looked into their eyes. Eyes like the early morning dew that glistened on the grass, like diamonds. They glowed with pride and happiness for their smallest and youngest friend.

Before he knew what was happening, Davey felt himself being hoisted on to the shoulders of the other boys. 'Three cheers for Davey!' they exclaimed. 'He did it at last. Hip-hip-hooray!' Now he was on top of the world.

A tear sneaked down Davey's face, almost invisible, like a thief in the night. Inside that tear was everything good: pride, joy, happiness, childhood fun. A tear of belonging, of fitting in. Conforming. Quickly, Davey wiped the tear from his delicate, velvety cheek, feeling the crowd move.

Behind them a small stream trickled through

the mud, overshadowed by an unimpressive, insignificant hill.

Silence. Only the trickling of the stream could be heard, through the woodlands and forestry. Somewhere there was a party, people shouting, dancing and drinking (too much). The grasslands turned into earth beneath the impact of their feet. Noise, invading the very being of the revellers and ravers. Blitzkrieg for the worms.

David embraced the noise, though the powerful, relentless thump was a source of pain. I feel, he considered, as though someone is attacking my brain with a hammer. But still he danced, and shouted and drank (too much). To be seventeen!

Then silence. The ruthless thump had taken up residence in David's head, like an unwelcome memory, but now all he could hear was the unassuming trickle of water. Smell the pine, feel that fresh, untainted forest air. It's wonderful. It's perfect.

And she was there.

'I've brought you here for a reason, David.'

David looked at Gill. She wore a silver dress, reflecting the subdued afternoon sun. Mousy blonde hair cascaded on to her shoulders, and her long, tanned legs were in full view. Moving closer, David's face appeared on the dress, though he was more interested in Gill's sublime chest. Even her voice made him a happy man.

'I want to break up.'

Like a drip slowly letting blood into a critical transfusion patient, David's life trickled down the lake. Suddenly, the forest didn't seem so beautiful. The sky was no longer a fiery red, rather a dark, raging blue. He was cold. And alone, so alone.

David cradled his head in his hands, felt his oily, spotty skin press against his palms. He was the mighty, and he had fallen so terrifically. Heaven trumpeted and rain fell from the skies, soothing the summer sores of the dry trees and plants. Water made contact with David's skin, rain from the dark, ugly clouds so far above him. Or was it maybe a tear?

'Come on, Dave. Smile, you're supposed to be happy. This is the last one – how about making it special by actually smiling.'

Dave was jolted from his thoughts by Stewart's piercing tones. He looked around, startled. It was a warm summer's day, the trees were green, birds were singing and the buzzing of tiny insects filled his ears. He felt the additional warmth of all of the people gathering round, felt their accumulated body heat. They were on a path, leading to a wonderfully gothic church. The cracked concrete under his feet was strewn with confetti, colourful like a rainbow.

Straight ahead of him was Stewart, disappearing under the black cloth of a large camera. A best man and a photographer rolled into one, he had joked to Sandra. Behind Stewart was a long field of grass, swaying slightly, and blurred by the heat. Miles away were hills, their place in his childhood fantasies still fresh in his mind.

Maybe one day I'll get there, thought Dave.

A tingling feeling alerted Dave to his left hand. Sandra. She was sliding sensuously into his grasp, her hand as smooth as silk and as soft as cotton wool. Then an adrenaline rush, triggered by the angelic smell of her perfume, always guaranteed to make him feel glad to be alive. He smiled.

Flash!

Dazed, the congregation staggered away, some forming smaller groups on the grass (swaying ever so slightly), others walking towards the church hall where refreshments were being served. The screams of children filled the heavy air, screams of fun and excitement, the constraints of behaviour and tidiness suddenly lifted. Gossip here, cool drink there, giggling everywhere. It was such a nice day.

Dave ran a sweaty hand through his greasy, dark brown hair. Then he put his head in his hands, overcome with emotion, or perhaps just protecting his pale skin from the sun. His face felt soft, sporadically pockmarked from an outburst of acne during his teenage years. He could feel the slight growth of stubble, although in ten years of shaving he still hadn't managed to cultivate a respectable beard.

Letting his hands fall to his side, Dave's eyes (watery and green) wandered over to his girlfriend . . . sorry, his wife. Wife! Who'd have thought that Sandra, with her understated intelligence, razor-sharp wit and supermodel looks – who'd have thought that she was his wife!

Next he looked at the children playing on the grass, some his nephews, some Sandra's. They all played together, recreating scenes from films and making as much noise as possible. They shouted at each other, but at least they were together, unlike the segregated adults. The joys of childhood, oh how he longed to embrace them!

'Play with us, Uncle David!' It was a niece, Claire, his brother's youngest daughter. She had mousy features and a small button nose. As pretty as a picture, everyone in the family thought so.

With a sigh, he sat down, bones cracking under the strain.

Sixty-five years have taken their strain on me, he thought as he sat in the wicker chair. A spasm of pain in his back caused him to wince. It hadn't always been like this.

When I was a child, I could run from one side of a field to the other, and still have the breath to shout to my friends. Now I can barely walk from one side of this room to the other, and I have to sit down for ten minutes just to regain the power of speech. The hand of God came down on me, and broke every bone in my body.

Young Davey had always wanted to be a film star, an action hero, someone who people could turn to in times of trouble. Now he was David, a miserable old man trapped inside his country house. Directly opposite his wicker chair was a log fire. David looked deep into the fire, tried to lose himself in the flames flickering erratically like Sandra's hair in the wind. But the fire was nearly out.

Sandra, the angel. David's eyes wandered to the mantelpiece above the fire. His wedding photograph, displayed proudly, as if it were the World Cup. Struggling against the constraints that his inner workings had placed upon him, David made his way to the photograph. Creaking, his bones or the bare, dusty wooden floorboards they moved upon.

Straight, blonde hair, now tangled and grey. Golden brown skin, now craggy and milk. Perfect poise, straight back, head held high. Now twisted, crooked spine, sprawled across a bed. Radiant smile, now loose, still lips, coated with saliva. Sandra.

* * *

It's a Compromise Anyway

A shrill, piercing cry from upstairs snapped Dave out of his reverie. He waited for Sandra to deal with the problem. But Sandra wasn't there, she was at her mother's, and Dave was alone. Warm, bare feet brushed against the fluffy carpet, tickling him. Dave made his way upstairs to deal with the problem. The problem was his bundle of joy.

Seven years of marriage. He and Sandra had almost given up hope, efforts unrewarded, feeling down. Then along came Melanie, baby, someone for Dave to cradle in his arms. Someone who needed him, who he needed. To give and receive love.

Still the cry went on. It dug into his brain, pecked at his mind. Reminded him of a party he had once gone to. Old friends, forgotten faces. That was in the past now. Now he was happy, not a film star or an action hero, but comfortable. And very happy.

Waaaaaaaagh! Waaaaaaaagh! Waaaaa–

Cch! Cch! Cch! Oooooooh . . .

The room was darker than charcoal. The night was colder than Pluto. The wind was wilder than a raging beast. And her face was blue, bluer than the deep blue ocean.

Before long, everyone was there. Neighbours, ambulancemen, paramedics. Sandra, her parents. His father. Everyone was there, offering help and advice and tissues and everything was going to be OK, fine, great, fabulous . . .

Melanie Curtis
Born 3rd April 2005
Died 15th October 2005
She who never was, never had a chance
Rest In Peace

The many winding corridors are stark, grey and empty. Outside, the wind has settled. Nothing moves, not the leaves on the trees nor the litter on the concrete. Baby has no rattle to play with. Somewhere, water is trickling through the mud. But not here. Here is peace.

An old man lies silently in his bed, reflecting on his life, or dreaming about what never was. Or maybe, as he tightens his grip on the quilt, he is just staring into the abyss.

A candle is burning on a nearby table. Wax should be dripping on to the table as the candle uses its tremendous power of fire to melt it. But it doesn't. Perhaps the fact that the light is dull, pale, limits the power of the candle.

Whoosh! A sudden wind springs up, charges through the corridor, though nobody seems to notice. They don't feel it, they certainly don't hear it. But the old man lets the covers drop to the ground, listens to the wind as it whispers in his ear.

Light. Burning a hole into the old man's retina.

But it doesn't hurt. Mother and father beckon to him, encourage him to come forward. Melanie cries. Sandra just smiles.

The candle burns out.

Smorgasbord

Leigh Debbage

Smorgasbord

The perfect pizza. The deepest of deep pan bases, garnished with lashings of the most exquisite tomato puree, dressed with four cheeses of the gods, platform to a generous topping of fresh tomato and thick pepperoni slices.

That very composition of divine piquancy graced the box that I, Lester Gaunt, was presented with at eight p.m. on Friday the thirty-first of March. The rules of Sammy's pizza delivery, however, forbade me from even opening the box.

Those not of the trade assume that pizza delivery boys dislike pizza, and that the act of handing such a delicacy to an undeserving, overpaying customer, after a journey with it attached to our bikes, taunted by its tempting aroma, is painless. Wrong! With a month's delivery experience behind me, one thing I had learned was that Sammy's delicious pizzas were not openly available. In fact, the only time we could enjoy their splendour was around midnight each night, when we had the privilege of devouring the cold leftovers, often after having to remove dirt and glass. I tended to decline. That disappointed me more than anything, considering the main reason I had applied for the job was not because it offered a hefty pay package – because, quite frankly, it didn't – but because I was as partial to Sammy's pizza as the next youth. More glamorous vacancies were available to an aspiring young entrepreneur: I could have been a paperboy or a cleaner, to name but a couple; but I had my heart, or stomach, set on pizza delivery.

With this thought in mind, perhaps you can begin to imagine the torment that I felt when Faustino the Falstaffian handed me Sammy's Pepperoni Smorgasbord with orders to deliver it to Donna Danson of thirteen Chelton Street.

'Mind 'ow you go – not exactly the nicest of areas,' he assured me, with a sly grin. 'Wouldn't want to lose one of our best delivery boys.' You knew he was being sarcastic even if you couldn't detect it in his tone, and the fact that they currently only had three delivery boys confirmed this. When he wrongly assumed that I was a suitable distance out of the door he bellowed, 'Hey, Sammy, Lester's off to Chelton Street!' This was punctuated with a round of irritating laughter from the kitchen, as he held his fourteen-inch belly in proud admiration of his prodigious wit. I didn't like Faustino.

The act of placing the Smorgasbord into the carrier at the rear of my bike brought a lump to my throat and a pained cry of protest from my dinner-less stomach (a hectic and miserable day had not allowed me this luxury). I wouldn't have minded if it had been a plain mozzarella or a Vegi Delight, but the Smorgasbord was different. The thought of riding with it so close to me, yet knowing that it could not be mine, that we would never be able to spend any valuable time together, reminded me too much of my earlier loss – my girlfriend suggesting that we 'just remain good friends'. I had managed to block it out up to this point, but as I released the pizza it all came flooding back.

I plugged my Discman headphones into my ears in an attempt to block out humanity, pressed play and hold, and concealed the plugs with my helmet, ready to listen to whatever CD happened to be in there. 'Boom Boom Boom!' wailed The Outhere Brothers, 'Now let me hear you say Waaiiooww!' A cold shiver ran from my head to the tips of my toes. I closed my eyes and groaned as I remembered that my eleven-year-old sister Janice had borrowed the Discman and had treated me to the melodic sublimity that was her All Time Bestest Album of All Time. Under the circumstances, however, I would have settled for anything, and with the volume near maximum I revved my bike to the tune of 'Boom Boom Boom' and left the parking lot in strangely high spirits. As I cruised down Victory Street I even found myself shouting, 'Waaiiooww!' in full voice, much to the consternation of the pedestrians. I can honestly say that I felt genuinely alive for the first time that day.

It was not to last.

Although I did not know Chelton Street, I was confident that I knew the general area and presumed that I would find it with little trouble. However, Sammy's ETA of eleven minutes past eight (his ETAs, like his pizzas, were precise) became more and more inaccurate, as The Outhere Brothers turned to Britney Spears and then to Bryan Adams. My initial irritation and hunger turned to exasperation and the warm, sweet-smelling zephyr from my rear became increasingly difficult to resist. I began to quiver with anguish. 'Surely Donna wouldn't notice if I just removed one slice,' I told myself, but as I approached the area where I guessed I would find Chelton Street, I held out against this temptation. I carefully searched the run-down streets, but to no avail. Elfin Road, Gordon Street, High Street, Sandy Close, then a strange sign that read *Welcome to* hel*l* – mainly written in black marker. An all-pervading stench enveloped this road, a combination of dirt, sewage and what seemed like rotting flesh. Many of the windows were boarded up and half the houses had clearly been uninhabited for some time. Every road had a similar appearance – battered, eerie, lifeless.

As the temperature of the Smorgasbord continued to fall and the temperature inside my helmet to rise, I reminded myself of a conversation I once had with Luke between deliveries, regarding the steady fall in the number of Sammy's delivery boys. He had taken me aside and told me horrific tales of violence, terror and deception as punishments for late deliveries. 'Of course, you know about the head clamp,' he wrongly assumed.

'The head clamp?' I nervously stuttered. He presumed I had heard the screams from the 'torture chamber' behind the kitchen where Sammy crushed the heads of employees as punishment for their unacceptable time-keeping.

'But worst of all,' he snarled, 'it is rumoured that some culprits, even younger than us, were strapped to a chair and force-fed a Texas Barbecue with green peppers and extra anchovies.'

I shuddered and nearly swerved into a parked car as Luke's voice echoed in my head. My stomach groaned with hunger. At the same time, however, I quivered to think of my punishment if Sammy discovered I had eaten some. Eventually, paranoia conceded to temptation; I stopped underneath a partially lit lamppost at the junction of an alley and burst into the barely lukewarm box. I knelt down and balanced it on my knee, then grasped the thick rim of the pizza with both hands, but paused when I realised that one whole missing segment would not go unnoticed. Without hesitation I reached for a piece of glass from the roadside and began to cut one of the segments in half.

Although barely warm, the first bite was the most succulent, flavoursome feeling ever to grace my mouth. Every muscle tensed with admiration. I wolfed the remainder of the minuscule slice and blobs of puree and loose cheese splashed against the sides of my mouth, but I resisted the temptation to lick them off. They would provide a welcome snack for later.

Then I came to my senses. As my left hand tried to steal the remainder of the segment, my right fought it off and attempted to squash the pieces back together, but as I closed one gap, other gaps were created. I bravely fought against the Smorgasbord but it began to deteriorate into a mess of stringy cheese, barely resembling the immaculate presentation that it had once been. 'I will not be defeated,' I told myself as I considered that the only possible solution would be to somehow fill the gap with something else. But where would I find bread, melted cheese and tomato in a hurry? And then a thought occurred to me: to compensate for a reduction in circumference I had to reduce the radius of the pizza. I thanked the heavens for my Maths GCSE grade D. Without further hesitation, I cut a mini pizza in the centre, both solving the problem and providing further morsels to satisfy my inexorable hunger. Result!

I covered the small gap in the middle with a slice of pepperoni then set on my way with a slightly smaller pizza (but let's be honest – who actually measures theirs?). With spirits lifted by my 'meal', I cruised to the end of Gordon Street, unaware that the real nightmare was yet to come.

Although the lack of life from the houses rather concerned me, I convinced myself that I was beginning to cover uncharted territory. Then it happened. Something nothing could have prepared me for. A noise that still rings in my head as I detail these events after weeks of therapy. Just when I thought it couldn't get any worse, 'Believe' by Cher screamed from my speakers, louder than before and more painful than the time my father danced to it at my brother's wedding.

I roared round the corners from road to road, only to find myself back on Gordon Street, then Elfin Road, then High Street, then once again I was welcomed to Hell. Cher's vocals echoed in my head as I skidded on litter and excrement, but somehow managed to keep my balance. As I rode down the frighteningly quiet Elfin Road yet again, now much darker and even more eerie than before, Cher wailed, 'Do yoeeuoo Beliieeiiiooiive . . .' in a distorted whine. I circled the maze aimlessly, hoping to bring this nightmare to a close . . .

Then, the final touch to a perfect journey. Cher began to repeat herself. Initially I thought it must be some infuriating dance remix as she persistently squealed, 'I really don't think you're strong enough!' for the fourth time, sounding even more distorted. Then it dawned on me that it was not going to stop. Someone had scratched the CD (probably in anger) and the same agonising noise continued to drill through me at amazing volume as I circled round the streets of the netherworld. I was convinced my head would explode.

Forgetting that 'hold' was activated, I frantically hit my jacket pocket with my left hand, searching for the stop button, while attempting to steady the bike.

A sudden swerve left on to High Street gave me another twenty seconds of straight road in which to fight the monotonous pounding in my combusting brain. I tugged at my throbbing helmet with both hands, but it was clamped firmly to my head. I ferociously yanked the headphone wires with my saturated palms, but they only ripped at my lobes, resulting in yet more agony. I veered into Sandy Close and, as the stench told me I was once again approaching the gates of Hell, my exasperation turned to hysteria, as I hurtled past wing mirrors and narrowly avoided lampposts. I would have stopped, but a small part of my brain convinced me that Chelton Street was just around the corner. 'I really don't think you're strong enough,' Cher persisted.

I pelted towards the junction of Hell, fighting my helmet with both hands, oblivious of the BMW emerging from Sandy Close. I spotted it little more than a metre in front of me. From then all I remember is a deafening crash, a high-pitched shriek, then blackness.

My eyes opened to darkness and silence. A soft pillow was cushioning my sweat-drenched head, but my bed seemed painfully hard. This was no way to start a new day; I would sleep again and wake after a good dream. A car door slammed and I realised my father must be leaving for work – that would give me ten minutes until my alarm.

I curled into a circle and rolled my head to the left. My pillow didn't usually squelch like that; curious. I sat up immediately to investigate; then it hit me. The stench of Hell brought me back to reality – this was no nightmare. The shining lights from the BMW helped focus my eyes. I noticed a white scratch, over a metre in length, running along the car, and a smashed window. The driver – about six feet tall, medium build, black suit – towered over me. From my inferior position his expression was hard to calculate: sympathetic or murderous? He coughed violently into a handkerchief, then scanned the area. I followed his eyes. Huge zombies, built like Titans, emerged from battered houses. They tilted slowly from side to side as they walked, with savage expressions on their grotesque faces. The crash had clearly woken them from their graves. Deafening thunder churned in the misty skies, echoing their groans. The driver stumbled away – this was no place for a businessman. He retreated into his car and hastily reversed out of the gates of hell. As the zombies returned to their houses as if nothing had happened, I looked around. The squashed Smorgasbord lay on the ground where my head had been, its topping scattered on the dirty road. Next to it was the sign, *Welcome to* hel*l*, partly buried in a small pile of litter.

I held my throbbing head and began to recall what had happened. Somehow I had managed to swerve to the left and the collision must have vaulted me, with the Smorgasbord, over the car's bonnet and on to the sign. Surrounded by blissful silence, in between groans of thunder, I realised Cher must have also suffered in the blow – a blessing in disguise.

I began to pick the pieces of topping up off the ground, convincing myself that if I returned it in the state that I was in, even Sammy would understand. I reached over for the furthest piece of pepperoni and then it struck me. The sign was staring right at me. Close up, I could see beyond the graffiti, and there, hidden amongst the dirt, were white shapes where the original letters had once been. I sank to the ground, supporting myself with both grazed hands, as the words *Chelton Street* stared back at me. It took no time to spot number thirteen – one of the few houses with its number still intact – as I picked up the remainder of the topping and arranged it in a reasonably presentable manner. Whatever the time, I would make this delivery.

Standing outside the battered terrace house, I caught my reflection in the dark windows. My hunched form looked ready to collapse, but that was not what shocked me most. My face was almost entirely blood red. However, my initial shock turned to relief when I scooped a tasty dollop of Smorgasbord topping off my left cheek.

'Can I help you, young man?' came a quiet voice from the doorstep. I turned to see an old woman, of gentle appearance, staring up at me. I produced the box from behind my back.

'Your pizza, madam. Sorry it's so late, the journey was a nightmare.'

'I had my pizza half an hour ago, son. Sammy sent me a replacement as soon as it was a minute late; he said he guessed you'd have trouble finding me. He's such a lovely man.'

'Oh,' I said, devastated.

'Perhaps you should have that – you look like you could use it.' I turned away, ready to collapse at any moment, but a smug grin began to spread itself spontaneously across my face.

'One more thing,' she called, 'I love the pizza make-up. I do hate delivery boys with no character.'

I leaned against Mrs Danson's wall and devoured

the cold pizza. I spared a thought for my fellow delivery boys who would soon be doing the same as I was with the leftovers back at the shop and I realised this was how it was destined to be. Eating Sammy's pizza would get no better than this. I enjoyed my full pizza while it lasted, then picked up my battered bike and slowly set off on the long trudge home, safe in the knowledge that I would probably make it back just in time for April Fools' Day. Fantastic.

Playing With Fate

Nikki Dudley

Playing With Fate

I hot-wired the car as my mate, Dan, kept watch by the passenger's door. His manner was alert and nervous, which created an uneasy atmosphere in the surroundings, aggravating me enough to make my hands slip from perspiration. Even though it was night-time it was easy to be caught, the dangerous silence definitely making it a bad night for crime. But I wasn't in any mood to be picky.

The engine roared abruptly and the sound was like a scream of our triumph as Dan clambered into the car. I gave him a small, reassuring smile as he reached for the door handle, casting a curious glance over his shoulder, reminding me that the danger was not yet over. In fact, it had hardly begun.

As I became familiar with the car – an automatic – Dan slammed his door shut. I cringed at the effect of the loud bang on the night's silence. He looked dazed as I threw him an irritated scowl, squeezing the steering wheel in vexation until my knuckles turned white.

I jammed my foot on the accelerator of the dark-coloured BMW and drove where the street took me. I hardly knew what I was doing but it felt good. Being bad always had been one of my favourite things, especially since nobody noticed anything I did. I saw Dan fidgeting uncomfortably in his seat. It was as if he had only just realised what he was doing, as if he had only just remembered our intentions.

The speed climbed in an instant: forty, fifty and sixty, almost seventy. It was dangerous but I seemed to be handling the car OK, even on the small back roads I had driven into. I hadn't driven much before, yet I imagined doing it wrong was exactly what I had in mind.

Then there was a flashing light; I glanced in the mirror to find a police car in pursuit. I was sure I'd enjoy the chase, and I vowed that the lonely car was going to regret even contemplating chasing me. The adrenaline I felt surging through my veins increased as I swerved round a corner, trying to throw off the police car. But I knew I would lose the car, I always had been one never to break a promise.

'Hey, Ben, they're gonna catch us!' Dan cried. I flashed him a look of annoyance and sighed.

'Relax, Danny boy, we'll be fine. I ain't been caught once, doing anything I do,' I told him, flooring the accelerator further.

I watched in the mirror as two more police cars joined the chase and I felt my confidence shatter. But I clutched on to the thread of hope that still lived inside me, never failing to rescue me. I could do this; I could do anything that I wanted to because I never had anyone to do things for me. All I needed was myself.

Two of the cars were dragging closer and I could see the passengers of the car on the right. One woman and a man, both quite young and eager to catch Dan and me. Someone had to win and this time there was no chance of negotiation.

I swerved unexpectedly, causing the car on the right to swerve as I did, but unlike me they couldn't control their car and they crashed into one of the road barriers. I looked back for a moment, overwhelmed with a strange feeling of satisfaction, and ablaze with pride.

I turned my attention back to the road ahead and gasped at the car headlights charging towards us. It seemed unwilling to budge as I stubbornly increased my speed. We were head on, both our headlights blinding the other. The car flew like an arrow closer and closer, its headlights devastating my vision but not causing my stubbornness to falter for a second. Dan was squeezing my arm, pleading with me to pull over and surrender but I ignored him. I never lost a fight. Never.

Beads of hot sweat slithered down my forehead as my anxiousness stabbed at my heart and pumped furiously through my every vein. The lights suddenly changed direction and I exhaled deeply in relief at the sight of the clear road ahead.

I glanced in the mirror to find three police cars still in pursuit. I should've given up but my determination was still burning inside me like a dominant flame. I wished I could've said that Dan didn't want to give up but I knew that he did. He was clinging to the car door for dear life and he had tensed up like a clam.

'Hey, Danny, lighten up!' I half shouted over the engine. But all Dan did was stare at me with his big blue eyes which now looked like those of a child, and they held such innocence it was untrue. That made me think for a second, but for no longer than that. I had no time to spare for conscience. As I turned a sharp corner, I knew there was no chance of getting off lightly now. Dan and I had broken too many rules. But rules were made to be broken. The temptation of corruption was too strong for me to resist.

The three police cars chasing us were closing in, limiting my chances of escape. One edged nearer and caught the bumper of our car but only pulled me off balance for a moment. I had to keep in control, it was the only control I had. My own life was completely unpredictable.

I had to increase the speed. One hundred miles per hour, and faster and faster. I was always the winner, I couldn't lose. I had to win this, if nothing else. I had to prove that I could do something, no matter what it was. I wasn't just a stupid kid like everyone thought.

I had something I could do and could succeed at.

They didn't give a damn anyhow. My dad wasn't even part of my life and my stupid mum was too wrapped up in her new boyfriend. It hurt that she loved him and not me. Well, forget her and forget being a loser.

The world was flying by; the speed of the car was escalating as if it would never stop. I could go on forever because I had nowhere to go, I had nothing to do. No one wanted me except the police officers who were following me now and that was for all the wrong reasons.

My vengeance and hate flowed freely right then. I could do anything. I was on top of the world and even the flashing lights that persisted in following me wouldn't change a thing. Yes, I was scared of the situation, but I was too far down in my desolate pit ever to resurface again. If I was going to lose, I was going to lose it all.

Then, Crash! I lost it all. I felt the pain before I heard the thundering crash that echoed in my mind. And I could hear the scream from Dan beside me; the guiltiness choked my heart almost into nothingness and tugged me down into another world. Darkness overwhelmed me and I felt like I was floating on air. Any sense of control was lost. Game over for me, the beating heart that had always been there had perished. I was dead, in a blaze of glory.

* * *

Anna threw the handset on the floor and rubbed her eyes in exhaustion. She always lost on that level! Her mum wandered in and gave her a sympathetic smile. 'Did you lose again?' she questioned, ruffling up Anna's hair.

'Yeah, I just looked away for a second . . . and then the driver crashed,' she explained and looked up at the screen, where the words Game Over bounced from side to side. She frowned again.

'Why don't you give it a rest?' Anna's mum asked and she nodded reluctantly. 'It's not fair though, Dad can pass all the levels.' She moaned and her mum took her by the hand and walked her to the door.

'I don't understand why you and Dad love the game so much. It's just about joy-riders, isn't it?'

'Don't start this again,' Anna told her mum and walked back into the room, turning off the TV and pulling the game Kamikaze Control out of the Nintendo machine.

Tam

Laura Gordon

Tam

'Typical,' Sophie muttered, half laughing but very annoyed as she climbed out of the car and pushed her short blonde hair behind her ears. In the middle of nowhere, between someplace unimportant and mount nonexistent, and they had forgotten their key. 'That's just fan-bloody-tastic.'

The six of them were down in Tam for a long weekend, because her father had been British ambassador in Algeria for three years now and even though it was virtually in their backyard, none of them had ever seen the desert. So as soon as Sophie and her brother Stephen had got home from boarding-school they had packed their bags again and jumped on a plane to take them the two thousand miles to Tamanrasset, complete with two bodyguards to protect her father from the dangers of the Situation which threatened at all times. Sophie knew little about it and cared less, for it affected her only in that it kept her cooped up in a gilded cage and far away from her friends and busy social life in England. Of course, there were compensations – the tanned bodyguard wearing shorts in December was one – but they never seemed to outweigh the down-sides, or to compensate her in any way for what she knew she was missing out on. Even this trip to the desert was scant consolation to Sophie, for she was a practical sort of person, grounded in solid reality, and the desert was the stuff of dreamers.

They had arrived in Tam the previous evening, and had checked into the one and only hotel after stepping over a drunkard in the doorway who was having a last drinking binge before Ramadan. The hotel was decorated in the fashion of the late sixties, but had the dingy, dated feel that comes between modernity and antiquity, and the long white corridors were filled throughout with silence. The six of them were the only guests, yet in the dining-room every table was laid. The silence was chilling, and every one of them could almost feel the presence of ghosts from the boom years of the last few decades, when this hotel had bristled with tourists visiting the desert.

The rest of the town was the same, as they found the next day when they took a chance by going to market. The windows of the Tourist Board of Algeria were dark and derelict as they stared down on the town from their previous position of importance, and there seemed to be numerous restaurants where no one ate, with a few people meandering aimlessly (although in Africa you could never tell who was wandering aimlessly and who was just taking their time going about their daily business). It was a far cry from the vital hive of activity that the town had once been.

When they got to the market they saw where all the people were, and Tam seemed briefly to be a thriving oasis town. The stalls were magnificent and varied, and as the family walked down the street their foreign looks meant they were immediately beset upon from all sides. A man selling long strips of indigo (Sophie's father told her that this was a type of Tuareg cloth which died your skin blue when you wore it), another selling heavy Tuareg jewellery, yet another with leather water carriers and camel-skin bags. Then further along, a woman holding out long strips of thin material for veils, her husband chattering excitedly and pointing to the black turban on his head (a *shesh* they called them down here), then stalls containing fruit and vegetables, and endless crates of dates. All around them people stared at their blond hair and Western clothes, calling out to them in Tuareg, Arabic and broken French. The six stared back, equally fascinated by the exotic atmosphere the place carried, then all at once burst into activity. Sophie's mother rummaged in the piles of brightly coloured veils, desperate for a souvenir ('It'll be so lovely for fancy dress,' she trilled, and sent Sophie's father off to negotiate for a *shesh*). Her brother was eyeing the dates with an absorbed look on his face, and the sexy bodyguard (whose name was Luke) had gone over to look for a present for his girlfriend. Sophie stood still, looking around her, confused by the unfamiliar sensation this place was arousing in her. A voice spoke beside her, and she spun round, startled.

'It's mind-blowing, isn't it?' It was the other bodyguard. Sophie knew his name was Ben, but she had never spoken to him properly before and was unsure as to what he meant, or how she should reply. As if sensing her dilemma, he continued, 'I mean the way they're so different, and yet to them we're the foreigners.'

Sophie had never thought about things like this before, and they didn't interest her now, so her reply was curt.

'I suppose so. I wasn't really thinking about that though.'

'Oh. What were you thinking about?'

'Nothing much. I was just enjoying the sun. So funny that it should be hot in December.'

Ben seemed to be about to reply, but her mother interrupted them. 'Sophie dear, do come over and choose a veil, they'd suit you so well.'

Oh God, how embarrassing. Sophie flushed red and went over, muttering to her mother that she did not want a stupid veil, comments which her mother dismissed immediately with the words, 'Nonsense, darling! Now come and choose one.'

The shopping done with a thoroughness that satisfied even Sophie's mother, they had piled into two cars and set off. Sophie had tried to engineer it so that she would be with Luke, but he was hustling her parents into the back car, so she cursed and went to the front car with Ben. Stephen had got there first so she ended up squashed in the middle, being thrown about every time the car went over a bump or turned a corner, ending up in a heap on either Stephen's or Ben's lap. Stephen was playing away excitedly on his Gameboy, and Ben seemed to be absorbed in some car magazine, so there was nothing left for Sophie to do but stare out of the window at the rocky peaks and flat plains they were crossing. Offhand she wondered what had happened to the sand-dunes she had seen in films, but it didn't worry her much – this desert was different, that was all, and it was no less beautiful or striking for that difference. Indeed, it was more so, for the craters and mountains surrounding them seemed like the surface of the moon, and no less desolate.

They had barely been on the road half an hour when Ben's radio crackled and announced that Sophie's mother had forgotten the key, so they tapped the driver on the shoulder and tried to tell him to stop. Eventually he got the message and pulled to a halt in the middle of the road. Not that niceties like that mattered in the middle of nowhere.

The second car stopped beside them and they all stuck their heads out of the windows to try and decide what to do. Eventually it was arranged that Luke would go back along with Sophie's father, and the rest of them would wait.

'Honestly,' continued Sophie, 'why does every single journey always have to go wrong? It could work out, but no, it just has to screw up for me. This is so annoying!'

'Ah, 'tisn't so bad. You've got to laugh,' Ben remarked by way of conciliation.

Sophie raised her head slowly and fixed him with a sarcastic glare. 'Would you like to explain what exactly is "not so bad" about the situation?'

'I mean, if everything went perfectly, we'd have nothing to laugh about. A perfect journey would be dull as shit.'

'If a journey was perfect, you'd have people to talk to who you could keep up some kind of functional conversation with, so you wouldn't need anything to go wrong.' She was getting more and more angry and was taking it out on him, aware she was over-reacting but unable to stop.

'That depends.'

'On what?' It was barely a question, but he answered her anyway.

'On how you define perfect, and how you define journey, and how you define perfect journey. I mean, the company isn't necessarily included in "journey".' He was irritatingly calm.

'A journey is a trip and everything connected with it. Perfect means nothing goes wrong. A perfect journey is a trip where nothing goes wrong,' snapped Sophie, and her eyes dared him to question her.

Ben raised his eyebrows at her tone, and wandered off a little way, staring into the distance at the dusty hills. Sophie was immediately overcome by feelings of guilt and went over to join him, standing beside him and staring where he was staring. He stood by the side of the road, the sun on his face, and in the bright light he seemed to be getting some kind of inner salvation from the view, but try as she might, Sophie could not see what it was that he saw – only a bleakly beautiful mountain – or gain what he was gaining from it. There was something there – she had never been so sure of anything in her life, but it lurked just beyond her sight, and with every frantic lunge it slipped further beyond her grasp. Eventually, after what seemed like aeons of silence, she spoke. 'It's beautiful, isn't it?' Tentative at first, she gained courage from the expression he turned towards her and went on, 'So beautiful and . . . and . . .' She was groping blindly for a word that would fit.

'And . . . ?' said Ben.

He was laughing at her, she knew it.

'Amazing,' she finished lamely. 'Look, I'm sorry about back there. I didn't mean to snap at you. It's just . . . hot.' There, she'd done it – and she hated apologising. Ben said nothing, which was almost a relief, but he smiled at her and she grinned back.

A few moments later the other car drove up and they set off again.

It took them five and a half hours to drive eighty-six kilometres to Assakrem, where they were spending the night, and for most of that time nobody in Sophie's car spoke except to ask the time, point out the occasional camel, or make some other equally mundane comment. After about half an hour Sophie gave up trying to think of interesting things to say and stared out of the window as well, drifting between mindless staring and deep contemplation. She had to know what it was that the mountains and the rocks and the sand meant to other people, for she felt she was missing out on something important, and she couldn't bear not to know what was going on. So she reached deep into the recesses of her mind to the places she had always buried and pondered what she found there, until she began to appreciate something – she did not know what, or if it was right, but it was something new and different, and once she had begun she could not help but go on.

She thought of all sorts of things during that journey – her life, Algiers and how, in some part of her, she always missed it when she was at school despite claiming to hate it, the desert and how much she loved this dusty bleakness. She realised why people were content to live here year after year even with the threat of droughts and starvation, and how it could not be right that she had so much while these people had so little, yet they seemed so much more content with their lot than their English counterparts. Above all she considered how she had lived her life without thought, and how she had sought to simplify and turn even the most complex of ideas into black and white.

These thoughts had not come to her of their own accord, but now they had been invited they flowed with the force of something that has been repressed and is now set free. At first she tried to control them but she had opened a floodgate that would not shut again in a hurry. They brought many mixed emotions, which she received with hope but not without fear, for she had never had thoughts like these before, and all strange things arouse suspicion, even when they come from within.

She sat motionless and stared at the passing landscape, watching as the shadows began to lengthen, slowly at first, then faster and faster, and unwillingly she was dragged back to reality. They must, at all costs, get to Assakrem before sunset – partly because the whole point of this outing was to see the sunset, but more importantly because there were no lights in the 'villa' (they all called it a villa, well aware that this was a euphemism for 'tumbledown shack' but still hopeful), and they had to get themselves sorted while the light was still good. The cars sped along, and Sophie was thrown around from side to side again, landing on Ben's lap several times and managing to distract him for long enough to start up a conversation. Nothing particularly mind-expanding, but at least they were talking. Eventually she plucked up the courage to ask him something that had been on her mind for the last five and a half hours – what had he been thinking about as he stared at the mountain? She peered towards him, her brow furrowing anxiously as she asked the question, eager to learn and eager that he, who had sparked everything off, should be the one to teach her.

'What do you mean?' he asked, puzzled. It seemed like an insult to Sophie – how could he have forgotten something so important to her in such a short time? She resisted the urge to get angry, but probed gently instead.

'You know, earlier, when they went back to get the key. You were staring at the mountain and you looked like you had some really profound thought thing going. I was just wondering what it was – like, if it was something specially exciting you wanted to tell me about.' God, she sounded like her mother.

'You mean the "beautiful and um . . . um . . . um amazing one"?'

'Don't take the piss,' she muttered. 'Yes, that one.'

'Can't think of anything in particular. I guess I was just enjoying the sun.'

Was he concealing his thoughts for some reason best known to himself? Sophie didn't think so – his voice had none of the guarded inflections of a man lying. Could he be teasing her, getting back at her for her dismissive comments in the marketplace? That was even less likely – he would only do that if he knew what she had been thinking as she asked the question, and there was no way he could have known. No, he had to be telling the truth, but she did not want to think about what that truth would mean.

Sophie didn't understand. Here she was, spoiling years of calm and mental serenity with hours of self analysis, all brought on just because some man had decided to enjoy the sun. Her anger boiled over, and although she hid it, resentment rankled. It did not occur to her that it was not his fault that she had mistaken his meaning, nor that perhaps she had been ready to open her mind and had just been waiting for a catalyst. All she thought was that Ben had tricked her, that he had deceived her into opening herself when she was perfectly happy closed. She felt violated, and her new-found knowledge hurt, like a dagger deep in her mind – a dagger that had been thrust there by a man she had trusted, who was now twisting it deeper and deeper and smiling at the pain it brought her. Now she felt, as she struggled to reverse the tide, that ignorance was bliss, and that she had bought awareness at a heavy price.

Departures

Jennifer Haddon

Departures

'The four minutes past five GNER service to Edinburgh will leave shortly from platform six.' Katherine paused to listen to where the train was stopping and once the list reached York she headed for the platform. With one last glance at the departures board as a final check, she boarded the train and found her pre-booked seat.

She settled down as the train pulled away from the platform. Gathering speed, it left the busy, grimy streets of London behind, so that it was soon rushing past endless fields. Gazing out of the window, she saw a dull autumn day, the sinking sun gradually draining the colour away from the landscape, until the countryside finally disappeared completely into the darkness. Still staring, she saw a haggard face, deeply etched with lines, the skin sallow and sagging. Age had not been kind to her and she thought to herself that it wouldn't be long until her time was over, and now she had nothing to keep her here.

The day had made her weary and she hadn't been sleeping well recently. Grief and the organisation of a funeral at the other end of the country left little time for fatigue. It was no surprise that Eric had wanted to be buried here at his family home, but with little family left, it had strained her somewhat. She wondered why they had never moved back in their retirement years. Eric's family home had almost become her own during their years of marriage. They had only moved away because of his job, and had always planned to return in retirement, but somehow the right moment never came. It seemed strange that she would probably never make the trip down to the south coast again. She was getting too old to be travelling across the country on her own.

She ran through in her mind what she had to do when she returned home: bank accounts to be closed; old friends to be written to, telling them of the sad news; legal documents to be dealt with. She almost began to forget that there would be no Eric there, no one to reach up into the high cupboards, no one to chat to while she washed up. Thinking of him and lulled by the gentle rocking of the train, she drifted slowly into a peaceful sleep.

She looked down into the open grave and watched as the coffin was slowly raised. The writing on the brass plate came closer and closer until once again it was readable: *Eric Clarke 1919–1999 Beloved husband and friend*. The vicar dusted the earth away and handed the small bunch of flowers back to Katherine. The pall-bearers lifted the coffin back on to their shoulders and began the slow march back to the church, the sharp black of their hats crisply outlined against the grey sky.

In the church again, she didn't hear what the vicar said. She knew it all already. She knew him better than anyone. As her eyes drifted around to the well-known nooks and crannies of the building, which seemed to radiate antiquity, she wondered who the long-gone people in the crypts were. She remembered all the times she had sat here, for weddings, christenings, Christmases, funerals and, of course, her own wedding. Finally the service was over and the hearse crept back up the road, along the same route that she and Eric had taken on the way to their wedding reception.

The automatic doors slid open silently and immediately the unmistakable smell of hospitals hit Katherine. She walked briskly down the anonymous white corridors. Each time she turned a corner she was greeted by the same white walls and polished grey floors. Her footsteps sounded clearly, echoing around the walls, and a metallic humming pervaded the building.

Finally she reached Eric's room, hesitating outside the door to compose herself and to prepare for the sight that awaited her. After a deep breath she went in to see Eric, now a cadaverous figure, pale and completely still. The doctor was already in the room and she nodded to him. Grave-faced, he crossed the room slowly, and firmly pressed a switch. At once the machines began to whir and hum, green lines once again tracing across the screens. Eric's chest began to rise and fall under the sheets.

Katherine stayed with him now, holding his hand, watching him as he became more and more like he used to be, until he woke up. Swinging his legs across the bed, he placed his feet on the floor. He offered both his hands to Katherine and she pulled him to his feet, agile and smiling as if they were both young again. They walked together out of the room and down the corridor. The walls now played back the scenes of her life. She saw briefly her mother and father, school days, college days, friends she had long since forgotten. The doors at the end of the corridor swung open and they came out on to the top of the clouds and into the sunlight.

'The half past ten train from London King's Cross has now arrived at platform two. This train terminates here. All change.'

Katherine was found there, sitting in her seat, her limp hands around her handbag which rested on her lap, and a faint smile on her face.

Relativity

Michael Hallsworth

Relativity

I was forced backwards, eyes bulging, chest constricting, as the whining started to pierce my skull. My neck was locked rigid, mouth pinned open. Couldn't move. An incredible burning pain, as if I'd eaten a burning hot potato, began swelling up my body into my brain. Jesus. I was screaming, sweat streaming, praying endlessly just for darkness to hit me. 'Seventy per cent velocity,' came the computer's distant voice, languidly drawing out its vowels like some good ole boy on a Tallahassee street corner. The whining built to a shriek, with objects doubling, tripling, stretching out, like constantly receding images caught between two mirrors, eternally reflected; they streamed, fusing into each other, until all I could see was a shaking blur. At the corners of my eyes, pulsing, flickering colours started to grow: purple, orange, blue, spreading across my vision, coalescing into pure white, the shrieking echoing in my ears as I gently spiralled away.

That's the way I remember the worst moment of my life. Of course, there have been plenty of other unpleasant moments (days, years), but they were more the result of suffocating inactivity, a kind of horrifying, remorseless emptiness rather than any kind of terror or physical pain. Maybe I should explain.

Einstein: that guy drove me mad. Literally. There's a famous example they use at Harvard to try to explain the theory of relativity (you've probably heard it already). There are two brothers: one goes into space and orbits the earth at the speed of light, never ageing, while the other stays on earth and becomes an old man.

I was the one who went into orbit.

Pretty good way to stop a conversation, huh? If I had anyone to talk to. Fortunately, in this place, no one minds you talking to yourself (in fact, they expect it). But I'm going too fast: let's start from the top.

OK, I was twenty-two, had done the whole Ivy League thing, straight out of Astrophysics class and into the Agency. But by this time NASA was practically on its knees through lack of money and just about everything else. They let me in on one condition – signing up for the SOLART project. How was I to know it would end up like this?

Everyone had heard about SOLART. It was NASA's last gamble, throwing everything it had into one mission, hoping to restore its Apollo glory. In the fifty-three years following the moon landings, the public had just gotten bored with the whole space exploration thing. Even the shock invention of a light-speed engine hadn't seemed important while half the world starved to death.

SOLART – Speed Of Light And Relativity Testing. The idea of changing the normal rules, of cheating time, death and all the other difficulties that we just have to put up with was something that could unite the whole world.

'The way forward, the path to the future, a true revolution affecting the whole of mankind . . . who knows, maybe time travel is nearly here?' Or maybe, as they sold it to me, all this was just 'Bullshit. We're trying to save our asses, not the goddam planet. This mission will buy us fifty years. Time travel, immortality – the big ideas – we leave all that kind of crap to the PR guys.' Welcome to NASA, 2022.

'You, Yates, are the luckiest guy alive. You'll be a national hero – an international hero, for Christ's sake. A pioneer. Name going down in history, the full treatment. You know, I have plenty of men who would kill to be in your shoes – and I mean that!' (I had to sit through half an hour of this.)

'OK, here's the deal. We've had our finest minds working on a craft for the last decade. The agency has just been waiting for the right pilot to turn up.' (An expendable one.) 'And we've managed to get some kind of stabiliser that'll hopefully stop you turning into strawberry jam when you hit light speed, heh.' Commander McKinley, he was a funny guy. Dead now.

'Don't worry – to you, this mission will be over in a second, and I mean that. You see, because you'll be travelling at light speed, time won't seem to pass. Fifty years'll go by on earth, but you'll still be twenty-two. We're gonna let you see the future!'

I couldn't back out. I had to leave my parents, who sure weren't going to be around when I got back. To me, it was as if they had died as soon as I left them: almost like I'd killed them. I'm sure I'll never forgive myself; sometimes I wonder if they did, either. I looked at all the photographs later, watched them grow greyer and thinner before my eyes – the two of them together at first, then, just Dad. All without me. Literally, my (unlived) life passed before my eyes. That first photograph of him on his own, shoulders suddenly hunched, somehow smaller, almost withered, made me realise what I had done. I'd created a life-sized void of unkept promises, of unfulfilled ambitions and unattended funerals. The constant presence of absence.

He had to deal with it himself, Frank, who'd been trapped in the Dakota bunker, told me. I thought the unspoken words – 'because you weren't there . . .' Maybe I could see resentment in his eyes in the later photos, or perhaps that's my guilt, reflected.

Relativity

And knowing that I would now only ever see my brother as an old man. Right there and then, I would have given away everything just to be an internet historian like Frank, and live out a stupid boring life, never becoming famous or rich or important. He was the lucky one. Being like everyone else: just normal.

The send-off from Gates Space Centre was pretty impressive, for a glorified guinea pig (and I'd like to see my facc on the cover of *Time* more often). I'll spare you a description of the take-off – you don't want to know about your gut being forced up into your throat, while your eyeballs try to find out what your brain looks like. You can imagine.

But the view was worth it: I can almost convince myself I'd do it again, just for that scene, that moment, where it seemed that there could be something to believe in. I'd got sick of astronauts' damn eulogies to the wonder that is Earth from space, but maybe I should have known I'd feel the same way. It's incredible. The thing that I remember most is its unreality: just like some kind of liquid painting, always shifting and fusing, set against the changeless glimmering stars. Alive, but unreal.

But after the fadeout . . . what? I'd love to tell you: it would probably answer a lot of tough questions. There's still a blankness in my mind, the kind of lost time you experience in dreams where, while you have forgotten time, you know vaguely that time hasn't forgotten you. But it wasn't like a dream. More like that weird state somewhere between being fully asleep and half awake. Where you can still hear things, but your mind can't make connections: the rain, trees, gunshots, a match being lit. Strange, isn't it, how you can never remember the moment just before your mind loses control completely?

Dark blurs began to smear across the whiteness. They thickened, resolved, and then rippled, as if underwater. The letters EREBUS. So this is Hell, I thought. But now the connections I had missed were reappearing. Erebus – a memory was struggling to break the water's surface. The craft . . . one of the heads of NASA had just heard that name and liked the sound of it. I don't think anyone knew what it meant, but it had stuck.

If I wasn't dead, then that was it. Mission accomplished. Adrenaline began flowing as I realised that it must be over. Just like they had said – travelling fifty years without even knowing it. I can't describe just how damn relieved I was – like my falling plane had suddenly levelled out. Relieved that I had got through it, somehow. Then came unease: what the hell was I going to find?

There was something smooth and hard at my back. I pushed down on my palms, and Erebus' cabin swung into view. It seemed identical to how I remembered it.

But something was worrying me. It wasn't the same. Something, I couldn't think what, was screaming at me from this room, warning me that something had altered, something was subtly, but devastatingly, wrong.

There were two levels to Erebus: this cabin, and storage. I did a mental checklist: the plastic command chair, the flashing bank of digital instruments, the food synthesizer, the hatch down to the next level, the . . .

The windows. The light, that was it. The windows were . . . blank. Brilliant white, like someone had painted over them.

A confused suspicion began to grow in my mind.

I wrenched myself off the floor and staggered across the cabin. I thrust my face towards the chronometer . . . and stared . . . the world falling away from me, hurtling and corkscrewing, as cold terror began to filter through my body.

They'd got it wrong.

Shit.

Time hadn't stopped – *it was running normally.*

And even as the panic started, hope was dying. I scrambled across to the coms board, desperately scrabbling at the radio switch. Dead. My legs crumpled and I was collapsing into the chair, staring and shaking. There were so many thoughts, I couldn't think. Until true realisation hit. The real horror of my situation crushed down on me – the unending crawling seconds, minutes, decades.

There was nothing in that damn ship. *Nothing*. It wasn't meant to be lived in! You try and imagine *fifty years* of emptiness – I, I couldn't age or even die . . . I was trapped in limbo, Purgatory, whatever. I'll have to roll out the cliché and call it 'a living hell'. But I can barely think about it, even now. Maybe that's the sedatives.

They tell me I went a bit crazy. Hey, who am I to disagree? I mean, who wouldn't? It was unimaginable. 'The horror, the horror,' as Mistah Kurtz would say. Conrad, I loved that guy. Read all his stories. Stop me if I'm getting too deep here, but I've always thought of my journey as like the one in *Heart of Darkness*. Only, I found the true evil in boredom. With nothing to do, your brain starts turning in on itself, picking up faults, convincing yourself that you're going over the edge. And once you start thinking that, the paranoia sets in. You drive yourself mad.

You know, I say fifty years, but time is strange. Sometimes the old feeling would come back from when I first hit light speed: I'd see everything stretch out and reflect, until I was pulled forward into the whirring tunnel. I'd wake up with months, even years just vanished. I reckon that's what finally unhinged me. Of course, I didn't know it at the time. There's nothing to judge yourself against, up there.

I returned to Iowa all that time ago – the vast plains curving around me, distant Shenandoah just a graze on the flawless horizon. Sitting on the porch steps, lying on the barn roof, watching the speck on the horizon become Dad on the harvester, backlit by the dipping sun's maroon light. The weight of the silence only lifted by flies droning lazily through the sky or a slight breeze rippling the great expanse of corn.

That was all you could hear at night – the sighing of the fields, waves on an ocean. That's what we were: isolated, stranded, marooned, with no way out. History's repeating itself.

A noise. Inside my head or not? Static.

'. . . sequence now commencing.'

It's a trick, has to be: I'd already heard that message before, echoing in my mind. But . . . movement. Shaking. The chronometer long smashed. It's not true.

But I realised it must be. Paralysed, I could see the light fading from the windows, to be replaced by . . . the starfield. To me, it was the most astounding sight you could ever imagine. I was shaking with fury. Where had it been before? Why hadn't I been able to see it?

What the hell had it done to me?

When the main door opened, I was hunched in the corner, clutching my knees up to my chin, shuddering. The sunlight, real light, blinded me. I heard concerned voices, real sound, thundering at me, through ears that were nearly deaf. Everything was alien – I was alien. I felt two hands pull at my wasted arms.

A wave of heat blasted out at me. I'd been deprived, hermetically sealed for decades, and I just couldn't cope. Outside was sickening. Overwhelming. The noise, light – so much . . . space. I started swaying and my eyes began to roll. Unbelievably, I wanted to get back inside. Fighting the urge to throw up, I squinted at the scene before me.

Thousands of people crowded around the landing site, whistling and clapping. Everyone looking at me. I couldn't handle that, after being alone for so long. The sunshine. The sky – I couldn't look at something so immense. It was dark orange. The sun was low, red and enormous, drooping over the horizon, hazy and shimmering through dusty air. It must've been touching a hundred degrees. I seemed to be in the bowl of a vast valley, surrounded by curves of sweeping rock. My shallow breathing started to catch on the air. This was Earth?

Relativity

I'm trying, but there's no way I can describe the experience the way it actually seemed to me, given the sheer panic I was feeling.

And repulsion. A man shoved his head near to mine. I saw him start at my emaciation and blank eyes, but recover quickly and confidently start to speak.

'Captain Louis Yates, welcome to Earth in 2072!' The guy had an accent I couldn't place, sort of American-English-French.

'We now have planet-wide link-up covering this pivotal moment in Earth's history. It looks like the ship and yourself have arrived . . . unharmed, but tell me – and the world: what was it like up there?'

I stared. What had it been like up there? Could words possibly be adequate to describe it?

A dig in the ribs from behind couldn't break my trance. What words? Could I even remember how to speak? Vaguely, I noticed the worried glances and the fading smile of the interviewer. I heard a ragged but worryingly calm whisper – shocked, I realised that this was my voice.

'In the void no one can hear you scream – no one could hear me scream . . . Or maybe you could . . . Why? It's not endless darkness you have to fear – it's endless light . . . strange, isn't it?!'

OK, I had really lost it.

I felt weightless, helpless, as a strange shaking laughter began to force itself out. The crowd had fallen silent and whispering. I was looking round wildly, the looming rocks sliding forward, the dying sun flooding towards me, drowning in a sea of burning light. Heels jolting down steel steps as they dragged me away.

And here I am, reduced to scrawling with goddam *crayons* on the back of an empty syringe packet. Staring at padded walls and bolted-down tables, at lobotomised freaks clutching at railings and America's finest psychos dismembering the furniture. And that's just the guards.

I'm an embarrassment to the government – they don't like failure, and they've done their best to deal with me. Slammed in a max-security asylum, nicely pumped full of morphine, addicted, not going to cause them any problems. It's all been neatly suppressed and forgotten – I saw my own funeral on the plasma screen a few years ago. Not that you can judge time in here. Sounds familiar? Yeah, I'm back in Erebus, staring at the floor, dragging myself through the years – except, hey, now I can die! I'm looking forward to that.

I'm locked away, but I'm not crazy any more. I'm cast adrift, alone, out of time. Ironic – being out of time is something I've never had to worry about. I've got decades of dead time just sitting in my brain – a whole fifty years' worth of nothing.

Einstein: that guy drove me mad. I told him so last week.

Out of Darkness

Edmund Hunt

Out of Darkness

A boy stood in the shade of the towering wall, his eyes narrowed against the glare of the sun as he surveyed the crowded street. By his feet was a large, battered leather suitcase, covered in grey dust from the busy road. Tourists dragging small children hurried past him on either side. Occasionally, muffled announcements echoed across the airport terminal. Cars and buses filled the road, stopping in front of the large revolving doors and sending out clouds of choking black smoke. Engines throbbed and roared, voices shouted and horns blared angrily.

Tired and bewildered, the boy heaved up his case and staggered towards an approaching bus. His mind felt numb from the stifling heat and tumultuous noise. The bus rattled to a stop. Dragging his case behind him, the boy stumbled across the litter-strewn pavement to where a queue of people was forming. The driver shouted something above the tumult, and the boy gave his destination. His hand searched his pocket for the cool yet unfamiliar coins, which he handed to the driver. People crowded the aisle, talking and laughing, heaving their bags into the wire luggage racks. The air was stifling and humid, and the boy felt a thin trickle of perspiration run down from his forehead. The bus juddered into life once more, causing the boy to lurch off-balance as he slid into a front seat.

The bus pulled away and began to climb up the steep road away from the airport. The boy sat with his forehead resting against the cool glass of the window, surveying the passing landscape as half-forgotten memories awakened in his head. Gnarled olive trees lined the white ribbon of the road. Clouds of dust billowed behind them as they passed tourists on bicycles and old men and women herding goats and cattle. The blinding brightness of the sun and the vivid blue of the sky gave everything a sense of unreality. The boy thought how beautiful it all looked, the paradise for which he had yearned for so long.

Its engine whining, the bus reached the crest of the hill. The tired passengers were suddenly bathed in bright sunlight. The bus jerked abruptly, and then stalled. Blinking, the boy gazed down upon rows of terraced fields, ending in a dazzling sweep of white sand. Beyond lay the glittering azure sea, merging in a haze with the cloud-scudded horizon. As he looked, he felt his mind drift back across a sea of cold grey years . . .

It was dark and musty under the tarpaulin. Water

washed softly against the creaking timbers. Dimly he could see the huddled silhouette of his mother, her arms drawn around the dark shapes of his two sisters. He could feel his grandmother's rough hands folded across his chest. His father coughed from somewhere close by. The boat chugged gently, and far away he heard the sonorous chimes of a church clock echoing across the water. There were the pungent smells of fish and salt water, and he shifted uncomfortably on the damp nets which covered the floor. He could hear the faint, muffled sound of his mother sobbing. Frightened, he pulled his grandmother's shawl over his head, breathing its familiar scent of perfume. He closed his eyes, as the lapping waves ebbed into silence . . .

An angry shout from the driver shattered the stillness as the bus roared into life and began to descend along the winding road. The boy gazed out to where a young child walked behind a couple of old goats. Tall date palms cast dappled, feathery shadows over the way ahead. As he surveyed the passing landscape, the boy felt content to remain on this journey for ever, as myriad scenes and vistas unfolded before his eyes. His thoughts turned once more to the distant past, as he pondered the strange events which had preceded that final boat journey. His mind skipped back effortlessly across the chasm of years . . .

* * *

Abruptly woken by a sharp whisper and shake of the shoulders, the boy yawned and opened bleary eyes. His mother's worried face, partly covered by a thick black scarf, peered over him. He struggled up, sliding out from under the sheets and slipping his bare feet on to the cool, wooden floor. Without a word, his mother handed him a bundle of clothes, furtively biting her lower lip. Bewildered, he stood and stared at her.

'Get dressed quickly,' she commanded as she left the room. Barely a couple of minutes had passed before there was the sound of feet ascending the wooden stairs and his father strode into the room. Swiftly he bent over to lift up the boy, carrying him down the stairs and out of the house. The night was cool, and a gentle breeze was blowing, causing the door to swing and creak. He was bundled into the waiting car. The engine roared into life, shattering the calm of the night. Beside him sat his grandmother and two sisters, cramped together on the back seat. The car bumped and rattled along narrow, winding roads. Unperturbed, the boy gazed out of the window to the silver moon which hung suspended over the brooding olive trees . . .

The boy was jolted awake as with a roar the bus juddered and throbbed into life. He was tired and confused. Memories crowded into his exhausted mind, each frozen event flickering over his consciousness.

110

Ghosts of dimly recalled faces floated into his thoughts. It had all been years ago, and he had been a child. He had never asked questions, content to let the past be forgotten as he quickly adapted to a new life. Now that he was returning, all the suppressed, unanswered questions rose clamouring to the surface . . .

The golden rays of the setting sun slanted through the window, casting long shadows across the dark beams of the ceiling. He lay back in his bed, pulling the sheet up under his chin, his gaze wandering over the shadows above him. From outside came the incessant chorus of cicadas and the distant calling of roosting birds. The shadows lengthened, and the golden light deepened to a warm red. Downstairs, he could hear the muffled voice of his father, raised and anxious-sounding. Occasionally came the softer, pleading tones of his mother. There was a noise from the doorway. Turning, the boy saw a tall figure standing under the lintel, his face catching the red glow from the window. He immediately recognised the brown, wrinkled face and gentle smile of his uncle. 'Goodbye,' whispered the man. After a stunned silence the boy cried out in a frightened wail. The figure left, and shortly afterwards the boy's grandmother bustled into the room. 'What's the matter, then?' she asked.

'There was a ghost,' the boy replied, his voice

faltering and thin. A worried expression flitted over his grandmother's face as she came and knelt beside the bed.

'Don't worry,' she whispered, removing the small gold crucifix from round her neck and placing it in his hand. 'Whatever happens, you'll be safe. Sleep now. You needn't be afraid of any ghosts . . .'

The engine subsided as the bus stopped in the centre of a small village. The doors of the bus opened, letting in a cool, fragrant breath of air. A man and a woman got off and stood by the side of the road, scrutinising a glossy map. Sounds of birdsong and of the distant bellowing of cattle seeped inside to replace the vacuum left by the intrusive roar of the bus. The boy watched idly as white flecks of dust danced in a slanting ray of sunlight that streamed through the window. Turning to look through the grimy glass, he let his gaze wander over the low, white houses which clustered around a small church. As he looked, he thought of another church, buried deeply in the distant recesses of his mind. He remembered that day when it all began; a small, insignificant event which marked the irrevocable future of an entire family. Memories of the past engulfed him once more . . .

* * *

Out of Darkness

The floor was cool and smooth. He lay back against the hard, polished leg of the table and made shapes out of a handful of small, coloured pebbles on the worn tiles. He looked up at his mother, her sleeves rolled up, kneading a ball of dough. In the corner of the white-washed room sat his grandmother, rocking gently and singing in her low, rasping voice. In her hands she held a turkey which she plucked slowly, the downy black feathers drifting to the ground to form a small mound. Orange flames flickered from the glowing embers of the fire, the only light in the darkening room. Steam drifted in thin wisps from a blackened cauldron suspended over the flames. Suddenly, his grandmother fell silent. There was the sound of someone crossing the room. He looked up to see the back of his father, bending low in front of the fire. A thin, yellow flame leaped up the fireplace, send-ing out a coiling plume of white smoke. The boy got to his feet and ran over to where his father sat. A photograph lay on the embers, curling and writhing as its edges flamed and charred. He watched in bewilderment as the faces of his aunt and uncle, framed against the white church, turned to ash.

The boy turned, looking up questioningly at his father, mother and grandmother in turn. None of them met his gaze, and each face was an expressionless mask. Frightened, the boy ran from the room. As he left, his grandmother called back to him, 'Your uncle is dead . . .'

* * *

The bus was gone in a flurry of biting grit and oily fumes. Coughing, the boy stood leaning against his case as the dust settled in a white haze over the road. Behind him, the sky was tinged with orange and gold as the falling sun dipped below distant hills. The roar of the bus faded into silence, replaced by the clamouring of birds and cicadas. Dropping the rucksack off his shoulder, he pulled out a crumpled sheet of paper on which an address was scrawled. The boy peered ahead, to where a small, overgrown track led to a cluster of farm buildings. He lifted up the lead weight of his suitcase and began to trudge along the track, his dragging feet scattering pebbles in front of him. He felt weak, tired and confused.

It had taken him some time to discover the truth. His uncle was a wanted man because of his anti-government stance. His parents, who had harboured him, fled rather than risk capture by the police. Only now that democracy had returned was it safe for him to revisit his country.

As he neared the whitewashed farmhouse, he could see warm light slanting through the cracks of the closed shutters. He quickened his pace, suddenly full of an overpowering feeling of excitement and nervousness. A chink of light was thrown across the courtyard as the main door was opened cautiously.

Laughter spilled out of the house into the night air. Outlined against the orange rectangle of the doorway stood a tall man, older, but unmistakably familiar. The boy broke into a run towards the smiling figure of his uncle. He had reached his destination.

Your Last Cigarette

Joanna Morris

Your Last Cigarette

The rain came down in straight lines. You saw it as an omen as you stared out at the lines of commuters on the highway, returning home to their microwave dinners and uncaring spouses.

Your last cigarette still expelled soft grey smoke, as it lay half stubbed out in a chipped china ashtray. The ice had melted in your gin and tonic and you could still taste the bitter spirit on your dry tongue.

The glow of the town over the hill turned the horizon orange as a thousand streetlights burned along a thousand wet streets. The rain was silent as it formed mirrored puddles on the pavement below your window.

You remembered a damp weekend at your grand-parents', twenty Christmases ago; the thoughtful present of a book you already had; the burned tinge of a flaming Christmas pudding and the silver six-pence you found in your first spoonful. That was the last winter your parents spent together with you. And as you lay awake, waiting for the man in the red suit to deliver a sockful of sweets and an orange in the heel, you could hear their argument in the next room – voices raised to accusatory shouts, the slam of a door and the creak of the sofa.

You remembered a long summer of swimming in rivers, sunburn and stolen kisses in the rape fields which gave you hay fever. The raised scar from skidding on gravel when you bent the front wheel of your bike remains on your knee. The sting of antiseptic contradicted the sweet consolations of a sugar lump and a coloured plaster.

You remembered the scorn of your mother when you were sent home from school. The thrill of sneaking behind the tennis courts for your first cigarette turned to young shame when you were caught. She had the same look a year later when you called for a lift home, green from vodka. And when she complained about your Ds which should have been As, you couldn't explain the shame of being unable to ask for help.

You remembered shyly holding the hand of the blonde-haired girl who let you kiss her, and you remembered how she let your friend kiss her too, and then how she danced with someone else.

You remembered your Saturday job cleaning at the big old house on the hill. And how your boss paid you extra if you stayed with her when her husband was away. You used the money to visit your father in the city to meet the woman he wanted you to call 'Mum'. You left while they were asleep and sat on the train home, scared of the man sitting opposite you, who talked to himself.

You remembered leaving home at eighteen and working in the restaurant where they spat in the food. You savoured those quiet nights, clearing up in the soft light of the table lamps when everyone had gone.

You remembered sharing your umbrella, waiting for the train, and the smile she gave you, and the sound of her voice when she thanked you. You remembered the times that followed, the smoky cinema, the Chinese take-away in the back of your car, the feel of her asleep beside you.

You remembered every second you spent with her. And you remembered the note she left, the note you still keep in a box under your bed. A thin apology and a harsh goodbye.

You remembered the cold funeral your mother refused to attend. The black coffin nailed shut and the finality of the vicar's words as he threw mud on to the lid. The lack of emotion that filled you as you lay the flowers you'd bought beneath your father's gravestone – the gravestone you'd never returned to.

You remembered moving South. The birthday cards and money that were the only contact with your mother, until three years later, when you received a letter from your aunt with a copy of the will. The junk your mother left you was sold and the last cord was severed.

You remembered the loneliness of the years, the

grinding routine and the dull existence of the city.

You remembered sitting in a church to get out of the rain and looking at the dark stained-glass windows, thinking there was nothing holy about coloured glass.

You remembered the decision you came to as you smoked your last cigarette and let the canned laughter of a game show drown out the noise of the traffic.

And you remembered each thing as your feet left the windowsill, your arms outstretched like a crucifix, in a perfect dive. Seventeen storeys of memories.

You remembered how far you'd travelled in your time and how it didn't mean a thing. You thought that finally, this was the perfect journey.

And when you hit the ground, you didn't feel a thing.

Who'd have thought that Chloë – cool, rich and so sophisticated – would have anything in common with Sinead, who longs for popularity?

And who'd have suspected the problems lurking beneath Jasmin's sparkling smile? And if we're talking about mysteries, then just who is Nick – the fit, supercool guy, but what is he hiding?

And what of Sanjay, who finds his computer so much more user-friendly than people? As five very different teenagers struggle to cope with their changing lives they fall into a friendship which surprises them all . . .

"*. . . five teenagers from very different backgrounds, the fun and drama of their lives is drawn with humour and sensitivity.*"
Pick of the Paperbacks – The Bookseller

Sunday 8.00 p.m.
Walking home, I said, "I don't
think he's that keen on her.
What sort of kiss do you think
it was? Was there actual lip
contact? Or was it lip to cheek,
or lip to corner of mouth?"

"I think it was lip to
corner of mouth, but maybe it
was lip to cheek?"

"It wasn't **full-frontal
snogging** though, was it?"

"No."

"I think she went for
full-frontal and he converted it into lip to corner of mouth . . ."

Saturday 6.58 p.m.
Lindsay was wearing a thong! I don't understand **thongs** –
what is the point of them? They just go up your bum, as
far as I can tell!

Wednesday 10.30 p.m.
Mrs Next Door complained that **Angus** has been frightening
their poodle again. He stalks it. I explained, "Well, he's a
Scottish wildcat, that's what they do. They stalk their prey.
I have tried to train him but he ate his lead."

*"This is very funny – very, very funny. I wish I had read this
when I was a teenager, it really is **very funny**."* Alan Davies

When Mr, 'hey, call me Dave'
Sissons suggests that 5B keep
a diary for a whole year,
reactions are decidedly mixed!
Yo! Diary! grants us exclusive
access to all areas of six very
different fifteen-year-old
minds:

Seb – the rebel and
'Spokesdood for a
generation';
Meera – a girl obsessed
with astrology;
Steven Stevens – so good
his parents named him twice;
Clare – the local neighbourhood Eco Warrior;
Mandy – Ms Personality and Karaoke Queen, and
Craig – convinced that he's the only virgin on the entire
planet.

Jonathan Meres has written a riveting and hilarious tale of
teenagers teetering on the edge of the millennium! It's a
story of changes, drama, love, intrigue and plenty of good
old angst! And that's just in the first week!

*"Meres' strong, irreverent characterisation and sharp humour
(he was a stand-up comedian with his own radio show) make
this a book that will achieve an effortless following."*
Publishing News

Laetitia Alexandra Rebecca Fitt has more problems than just an odd name. Like three younger brothers (euk!), a baby sister, and an older sister with very strong views on life (Alex's). Having crazily busy parents may mean freedom – which is cool – but it also means they never notice Alex. Added to this, the love of Alex's life (Kevin in Year 12) doesn't know she exists. And then there's friends and parties . . .

By the author of the *Help!* series: *Help! My Family is Driving Me Crazy!*, *Help! My Social Life is a Mess!* and *Help! Let Me Out of Here!* and of the titles *Boywatching!*, *Girls are From Saturn Boys are From Jupiter* and *How to be Completely Cool*.

If you would like more information about
books available from Piccadilly Press and how
to order them, please contact us at:

Piccadilly Press Ltd.
5 Castle Road
London
NW1 8PR

Tel: 020 7267 4492
Fax: 020 7267 4493